Merv and Brian and The Chopper.

By

John C Burt

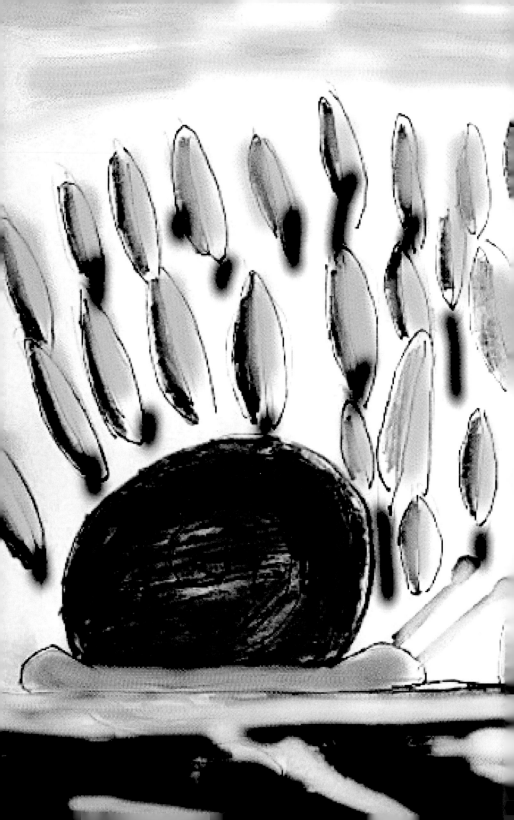

This is a story about Merv and Brian the snail and the chopper that comes down in the vegetable garden of Merv ....

Merv's vegetable garden had thus far survived the attentions of Brian the snail ..... Brian had not eaten everything in Merv's garden as yet ..... But he had tried rather unsuccessfully to eat some of Merv's vegetables.......

One cold, very cold and very windy day a chopper was flying above Merv's vegetable garden ....

The chopper was so low that Merv's vegetables were being blown about by the rushing wind caused by the chopper ....

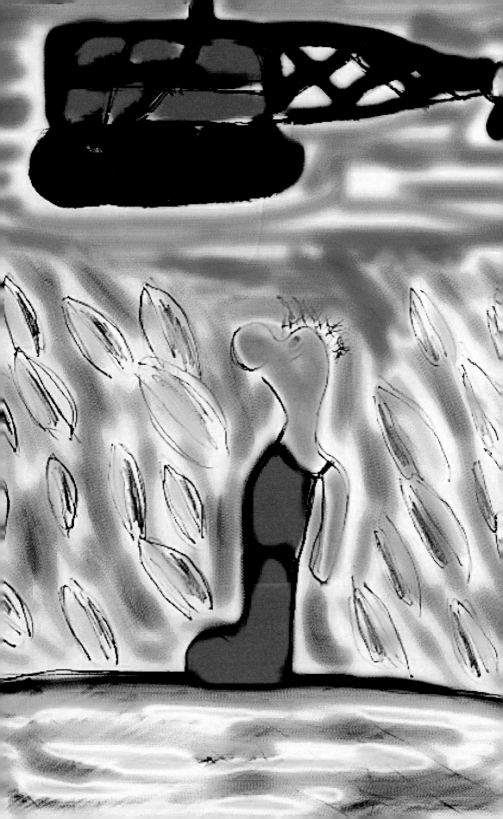

Merv thought his plants had survived without too much trouble ....
Then the chopper was struck by two bolts of lightning and had

to come down in Merv's vegetable garden .....

Some of the plants were destroyed but Merv was more concerned with the chopper pilot.

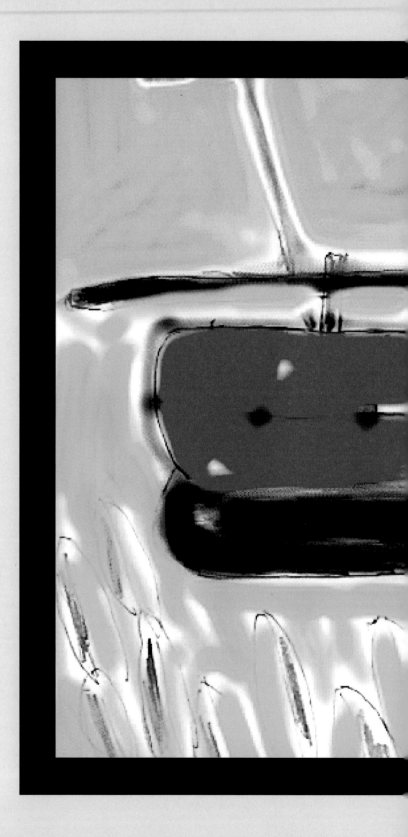

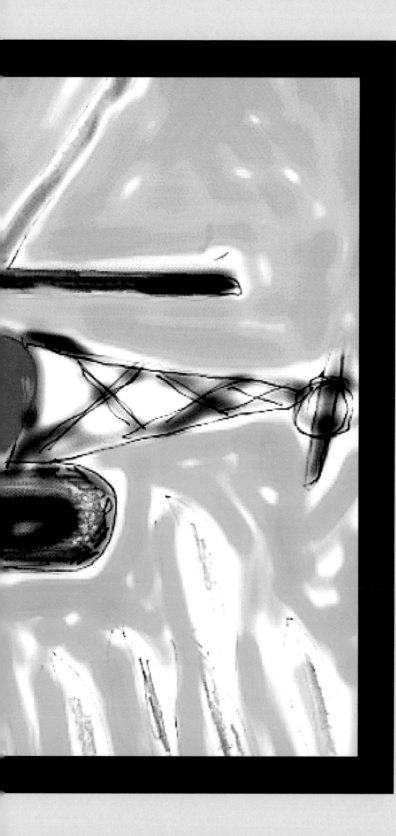

Merv now had a very important phone call to make? He had to ring the chopper repair service for the pilot ....

Merv and the pilot were both hoping the repair van would arrive quickly ....

The pilot was eager to finish his flight in the

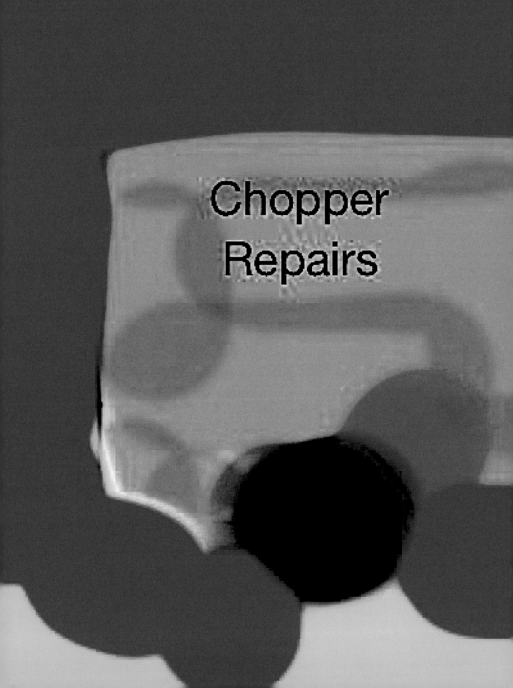

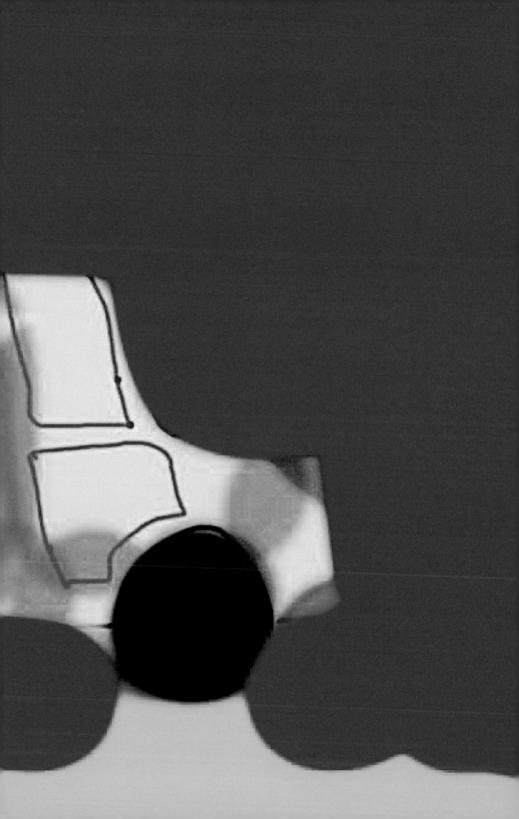

chopper ...
   The service van arrived in good time .... The repairs were made to the chopper and it was soon ready to fly again .... up, up ,

and away into the wild blue yonder......Or so the pilot of the chopper thought to himself ....He was looking forward to being

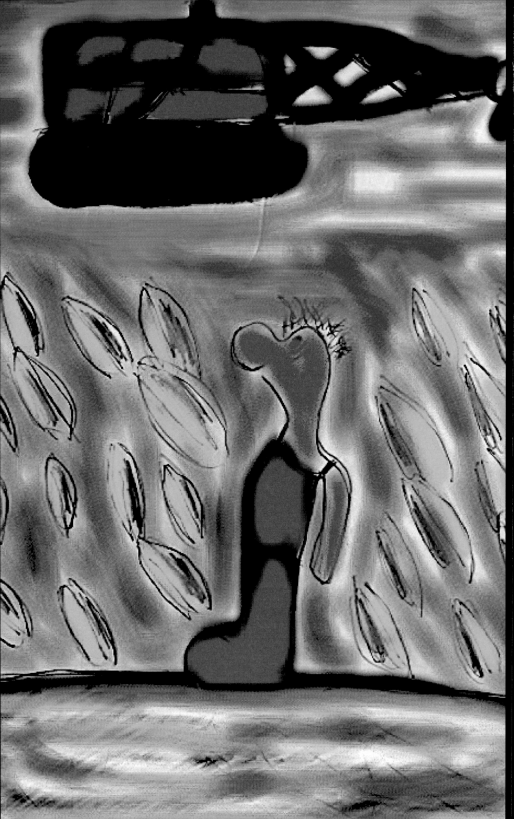

back in the air ...
Also Merv was
not too sad when
the chopper
finally lifted off the
ground again
...leaving his
garden in peace ..

So as the chopper departed the scene .... Merv was left with his old friend Brian the Snail .... and of course his vegetable garden.......

The vegetable garden was now a sorry sight for Merv's eyes .... He almost could not bear to look at the garden anymore ...... What was to become of it ?

In spring Merv planted new plants and seedlings and they took off .... Soon Merv's garden was back to looking its best.

Merv this time around planted the plants closer together ..... Just in case another chopper decided to drop into his garden again?

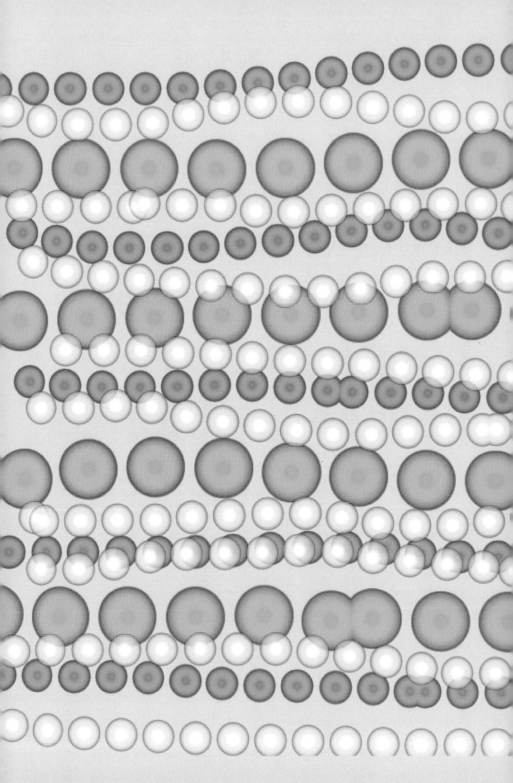

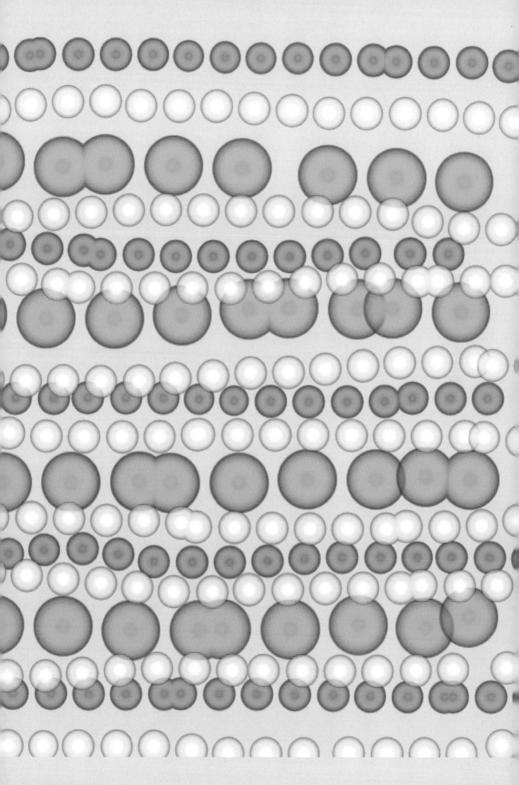